WELCOME TO SHANNA'S First Readers

Each **Level 1 Shanna First Reader** features:

- rhyme and rhythm
- picture clues
- easy words
- sight words
- phonics games
- large print

As children learn to read, they are most successful with books that feature rhyme and rhythm, repetition of words, predictable language, and decodable words. These elements are all "clues" that children use to sound out, read, and recognize new words. Below are some ways to utilize these "clues" with your child as you read **Shanna's Party Surprise** together!

Repetition Clues Look for words like *Hurry, hurry!* that are repeated a few times. If you read the first *Hurry!* your child may be able to read the others.

Rhythm and Rhyme Clues Children love rhythm and rhyme, and these features help them read. Anticipating a rhyme because of the rhythm helps children sound out words. The rhyme is a clue to the sound. While reading, pause to allow your child time to fill in the rhyming words throughout the story.

Phonics Clues If your child knows that the sound for the letter *R* can be "rrr," the sound for the letter *E* can be "eh," and the sound for D is "duh," then your child may be able to link the three sounds together and read *Red*. You can help your child sound out words this way. But a word of caution: don't overdo it. Catching on to phonics is developmental. It happens when it happens—like walking and talking. Your job is to coach cheerfully and patiently. One appropriate phonics reading game you can play is to look for words that are similar. For example, you might ask, "How do the words *Yum* and *Yummy* look and sound alike?"

Story Clues The more your child hears this story, the better equipped your child will be to read it. Just knowing what's coming next helps your child figure out which words are appropriate and which don't make sense.

Picture Clues Encourage your child to use the pictures in the story as clues to identify or rhyme a new word.

Happy Reading!
Jean Marzollo

For Imani Rae Prince

**Special thanks to Jackie Carter,
Editorial Director of Jump at the Sun,
for her commitment to helping children
learn to read enjoyably**

For information please address Hyperion Books for Children, 114 Fifth Avenue, New York, New York 10011-5690.

Printed in the United States of America

First Edition
1 3 5 7 9 10 8 6 4 2

Library of Congress
Cataloging-in-Publication Data on file.
ISBN 0-7868-1828-X

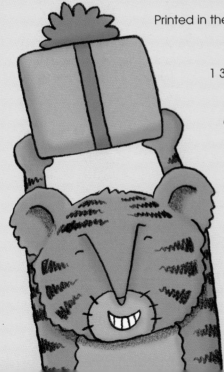

Visit www.hyperionbooksforchildren.com

LEVEL 1

Shanna's FIRST READERS

Shanna's Party Surprise

By Jean Marzollo

Based on art by Shane W. Evans
Illustrated by Maryn Roos

Jump at the Sun/Hyperion Books for Children • New York

Yellow hats,
too!

Orange presents, too!

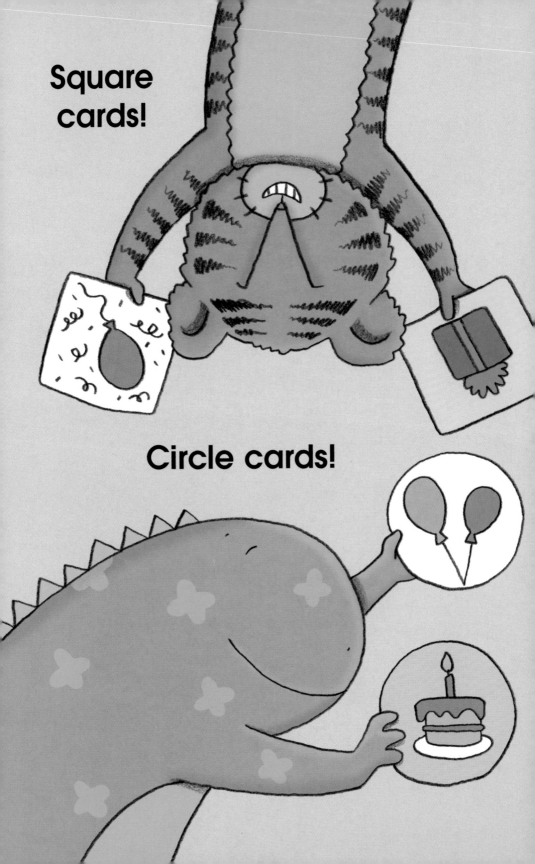

Square
cards!

Circle cards!

Triangle,
too!

RISE!!

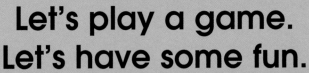

Let's play a game.
Let's have some fun.

SHANE'S TREASURE HUNT

2 red hats

2 blue hats

2 green presents

2 purple presents

2 orange presents

3 square cards

3 circle cards

1 triangle card

Find these treasures one by one.

SHANE'S TREASURE HUNT

- 2 red hats
- 2 blue hats
- 2 green presents
- 2 purple presents
- 2 orange presents
- 3 square cards
- 3 circle cards
- 1 triangle card

Happy Birthday, Shane!

Thank you, Dinah!
Thank you, Shanna!
Thank you, Ducky!
Thank you, Tiger!

Shanna's Matching Game

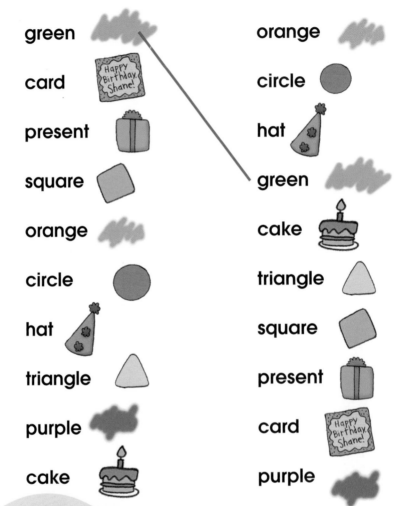

green

card

present

square

orange

circle

hat

triangle

purple

cake

orange

circle

hat

green

cake

triangle

square

present

card

purple

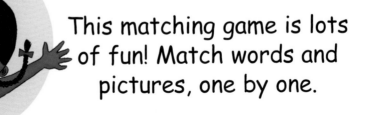

This matching game is lots of fun! Match words and pictures, one by one.